Thomas the Tank Engine & Friends

A BRITT ALLCROFT COMPANY PRODUCTION

Based on The Railway Series by The Rev W Awdry
© Gullane (Thomas) LLC 2002

Visit the Thomas & Friends web site at www.thomasthetankengine.com

ISBN 0-439-33841-7

12 11 10 9 8 7 6 5 4 3 2 1   2 3 4 5 6 7/0
Printed in the U.S.A.
First Scholastic printing, January 2002

Down the Mine

by
The REV. W. AWDRY

SCHOLASTIC INC.

New York   Toronto   London   Auckland   Sydney
Mexico City   New Delhi   Hong Kong   Buenos Aires

One day, Thomas was at the junction when Gordon shuffled in with some freight cars.

"*Poof!*" remarked Thomas, "what a funny smell! Can you smell a smell?"

"I can't smell a smell," said Annie and Clarabel.

"A funny, musty sort of smell," said Thomas.

"No one noticed it till you did," grunted Gordon. "It must be yours."

"Annie! Clarabel! Do you know what I think it is?" whispered Thomas loudly. "It's ditch water!"

Gordon snorted, but before he could answer, Thomas puffed away quickly.

Annie and Clarabel could hardly believe their ears!

"He's *dreadfully* rude; I feel quite ashamed." "I feel *quite* ashamed, he's dreadfully rude," they twittered to each other.

"You mustn't be rude, you make us ashamed," they kept telling Thomas.

But Thomas didn't care a bit.

"That was funny, that was funny," he chuckled. He felt very pleased with himself.

Annie and Clarabel were deeply shocked. They had great respect for Gordon the Big Engine.

Thomas left the coaches at a station and went to a mine for some freight cars.

Long ago, Miners, digging for lead, had made tunnels under the ground.

Though strong enough to hold up freight cars, their roofs could not bear the weight of engines.

A large notice said: DANGER. ENGINES MUST NOT PASS THIS BOARD. Thomas had often been warned, but he didn't care.

Silly old board, he thought. He had often tried to pass it, but had never succeeded.

This morning he laughed as he puffed along. He had made a plan.

He had to push empty freight cars into one siding and pull out full ones from another.

His Driver stopped him, and the Fireman went to turn the points.

"Come on," waved the Fireman, and they started.

The Driver leaned out of the cab to see where they were going.

Now! said Thomas to himself, and, bumping the freight cars fiercely, he jerked his Driver off the footplate.

"Hurrah!" laughed Thomas, and he followed the freight cars into the siding.

"Stupid old board!" said Thomas as he passed it. "There's no danger; there's no danger."

His Driver, unhurt, jumped up. "Look out!" he shouted.

The Fireman clambered into the cab. Thomas squealed crossly as his brakes were applied.

"It's quite safe," he hissed.

"Come back," yelled the Driver, but before they could move, there was a rumbling and the rails quivered.

The Fireman jumped clear. As he did so the ballast skipped away and the rails sagged and broke.

"Fire and Smoke!" said Thomas, "I'm sunk"—and he was!

Thomas could just see out of the hole, but he couldn't move.

"Oh dear!" he said, "I am a silly engine."

"And a very naughty one, too," said a voice behind him, "I saw you."

"Please get me out; I won't be naughty again."

"I'm not so sure," replied Sir Topham Hatt. "We can't lift you out with a crane, the ground's not firm enough. Hm . . . Let me see . . . I wonder if Gordon could pull you out."

"Yes, Sir," said Thomas nervously. He didn't want to meet Gordon just yet!

"Down a mine is he? Ho! Ho! Ho!" laughed Gordon.

"What a joke! What a joke!" he chortled, puffing to the rescue.

"*Poop! Poop!* Little Thomas," he whistled, "we'll have you out in a couple of puffs."

Strong cables were fastened between the two engines.

"*Poop! Poop! Poop!*"

"Are you ready? *HEAVE!*" called Sir Topham Hatt.

But they didn't pull Thomas out in two puffs; Gordon was panting hard and nearly purple before he had dragged Thomas out of the hole, and safely past the board.

"I'm sorry I was cheeky," said Thomas.

"That's all right, Thomas. You made me laugh. I like that. I'm in disgrace," Gordon went on pathetically, "I feel very low."

"I'm in disgrace, too," said Thomas.

"Why! So you are Thomas; we're both in disgrace. Shall we form an Alliance?

"An Ally—what—was—that?"

"An Alliance, Thomas, 'United we stand, together we fall,'" said Gordon grandly. "You help me, and I help you. How about it?"

"Right you are," said Thomas.

"Good! That's settled," rumbled Gordon.

And buffer to buffer the Allies puffed home.

Now flip the book over to start another Thomas & Friends adventure.